Me, Hailey!

By Sheri Plucker
Illustrated by Todd Fargo

Jason and Nordic Publishers
Hollidaysburg, Pennsylvania

Me, Hailey!

Library of Congress Cataloging-in-Publication Data

Plucker, Sheri, 1970-
    Me, Hailey! /by Sheri Plucker ; illustrated by Todd Fargo.
        p. cm.— (Turtle books)
    Summary: An understanding teacher helps her students welcome
Hailey, a five-year-old with Down syndrome who is excited about
starting kindergarten.
        ISBN 0-944727-50-6 (lib. Bdg.:alk. Paper)—-ISBN 0-944727-49-2
    (pbk.:alk. Paper)
        [1. Down syndrome—Fiction. 2.People with mental disabilities—
Fiction. 3. First day of school—Fiction. 4. Kindergarten—Fiction. 5.
Schools—Fiction.] 1. Fargo, Todd, 1963-ill. II. Title. III. Series.

PZ7.P282Me 2005
[E] —dc22   2005043383

                ISBN 0-944727-50-6 Library binding
                ISBN 0-944727-49-2 Perfect paper binding

            Printed in the United States of America
                    On acid free paper

For my children,

Brennen, Peyton and Hailey

and
to all the special children who
have touched the lives of
others.

Hailey opened her eyes and remembered! She popped out of bed, ran to the closet and picked out her pretty pink shirt. Soon she was dressed.

"Pancakes!" cried Hailey as she ran into
the kitchen and climbed into her chair.
"Yummy!" she said and syrup dripped
onto her chin.

When she finished her last bite, she
hurried down the hall to brush her teeth.
Then she grabbed her backpack and
plopped down by the front door to wait.
"Hailey ready now," she called.

Mom peeked around the corner. "Hailey, where are your glasses?"

Hailey reached into her pocket, pulled out her glasses and pushed them on her nose. "Hailey ready now!" she said.

At last Mom called, "Time to go."

Hailey jumped to her feet and ran ahead to the bus stop.

The bus roared around the corner and stopped. Hailey hugged her Mom and climbed the tall steps.

"One, two," Hailey counted as she
walked by each seat. "Three, four..."

"Five," said a girl with brown pigtails
and a big smile. "Your pink shirt looks just
like mine. Sit with me! My name's Sarah."

Hailey sat down next to her.

"Me, Hailey," she said.

Sarah and Hailey sang silly songs and talked all the way to school.

When the bus stopped, a helper met them and walked them to their room.

They were in the same room!

"Good morning. I'm Mrs. Carlson," the teacher said. "And your names are?"

"Me, Hailey," and "Sarah," the girls
answered together.

"Well, Hailey and Sarah, here are your
name tags. Find one just like yours and
you have found your seat."

Hailey smiled her biggest smile as she
marched around the tables. "Hi, girl. Hi,
boy," she said. Sarah followed, until they
found their name cards on the tables.

"Good morning, boys and girls!" Mrs. Carlson said.

"Good morning, Mrs. Carlson."

Mrs. Carlson smiled. "When I read your name, please raise your hand and say 'here'." She checked off each name from her list. Finally, she read, "Hailey?"

Hailey stood and waved her hand in the air. "Me, Hailey! H-a-i-l-e-y," she said and walked to the front of the room.

Mrs. Carlson led her back to her seat.

"Why did she do that?" Joey asked.

Mrs. Carlson smiled. "Hailey has Down syndrome. This means she looks a little different and learns a little slower. She may need some of you to be her helpers."

"Right now, it's circle time." Mrs. Carlson looked around. "Hailey, where are your glasses?"

"Here they are," Sarah yelled and gave Hailey her glasses.

Hailey pushed her glasses on her nose. "Hailey ready now!"

"**Now** it's circle time," Mrs. Carlson said. The children quickly found places around Mrs. Carlson's chair. As she began singing the alphabet song, Hailey started to sing and move her fingers.

"What's Hailey doing?" Joey asked.

Mrs. Carlson smiled. "She uses signs to help her talk. Let's see if we can learn it, too. Hailey, come stand next to me," said Mrs. Carlson. "Can you help teach us the signs for the alphabet?"

The children wiggled their fingers to make each letter.

When the song ended, Joey lifted two thumbs up, "That's so cool!"

Mrs. Carlson said. "All those wearing blue may line up at the door. Line up if you're wearing another color!" The children laughed and lined up at the door. "Now we're ready for recess!"

"Hailey, where are your glasses?" Mrs. Carlson asked.

"I know," Joey called and ran to the book table. He held up Hailey's glasses.

Hailey pushed them on her nose. "Hailey ready now!"

"**Now** we're ready for recess. Be very quiet and follow me," Mrs. Carlson said.

Suddenly, Jenny tripped over her
shoelace and fell. "Ouch," she cried.

"Help you," Hailey grabbed Jenny's arm
and pulled her up. "You okay?" she asked.

Jenny smiled, "I'm OK. Thanks!"

The girls hurried to catch up.

Outside, they ran to the swings. Hailey placed her tummy on a swing. Jenny took the next swing. They pushed off with their feet, and sang songs as the wind blew on their faces.

When the bell rang, the children all raced to be first in line.

"Inside voices," Mrs. Carlson said and opened the door.

"Hailey, glasses?" Mrs. Carlson asked.

Hailey reached into her pocket and pulled out her glasses. She pushed them on her nose. "Hailey ready now!"

They walked quietly back to the room.

"Let's think about our day," Mrs.
Carlson said. "Raise your hand if you met
a new friend today."

"I met Hailey," Sarah said.

"Great!" Mrs. Carlson said.

"Who had fun doing something new today?" Mrs. Carlson asked.

"Hailey showed us how to sign the ABC's. That was fun, " Joey said.

"Fun!" "Yes!" the children answered. Mrs. Carlson agreed.

"Clap your hands if you loved recess," said Mrs. Carlson.

All the children clapped their hands.

Jenny raised her hand. "Hailey helped me when I fell," she said.

Mrs. Carlson smiled, "Wow! Hailey, you've been a busy helper today!"

Mrs. Carlson stood up. "Who wants to go home?"

All the hands waved wildly.

Mrs. Carlson laughed. "Let's get our things together so we can go home." Mrs. Carlson looked at Hailey. "Hailey, where are your glasses?"

Hailey placed her finger on her chin. "Hmm, I don't know," she said.

"I need helpers! Hailey has lost her glasses again."

The children jumped to their feet and began the search.

Joey looked on the book table. They weren't there.

Jenny looked in Hailey's backpack. They weren't there.

Sarah and Hailey sat together quietly in the front seat of the bus. When the bus pulled to a stop, Hailey climbed down and ran into her Mom's arms.

"How was your day, Hailey?"

Hailey laughed. "Played on swings... friends. Hailey teach ABC's."

Mom smiled. "It sounds like you've had a busy day."

As they walked home holding hands, Mom said, "I'm so glad you left your glasses on all day!"

Hailey smiled and pushed her glasses up on her nose.